"Wait, I Have a Story About That."

(Anecdotes for my son from 25 years of advising financially troubled companies)

By
Mike Policano

iUniverse, Inc.
New York   Bloomington

Wait, I Have a Story About That.

(Anecdotes for my son from 25 years of advising financially troubled companies)

iUniverse books may be ordered through booksellers or by contacting:

iUniverse
1663 Liberty Drive
Bloomington, IN 47403
www.iuniverse.com
1-800-Authors (1-800-288-4677)

Because of the dynamic nature of the Internet, any Web addresses or links contained in this book may have changed since publication and may no longer be valid. The views expressed in this work are solely those of the author and do not necessarily refl ect the views of the publisher, and the publisher hereby disclaims any responsibility for them.

This is a work of fiction. All of the characters, names, incidents, organizations, and dialogue in these short stories are either the products of the author's imagination or are used fictitiously.

ISBN: 978-0-595-49625-9 (pbk)
ISBN: 978-0-595-61181-2 (ebk)

Printed in the United States of America

THIS BOOK

This book started as a collection of stories and comments for my son, Dave. However, a few people suggested that others might also enjoy reading this book. I will not mention their names in order to protect them from your wrath.

I submit this book to you for your enjoyment and thought. I have another 100+ items to write about. I have decided to get this book out without them. If you all decide this book is a worthwhile read, then I will write the other items in another book.

If you think this book is a complete waste of time, the next book will go to a different group.

If you enjoy this book, I respectfully request that you consider making a donation to TeamLuke, 233A Rock Road, #350, Glen Rock, NJ 07452

Please refer to www.teamluke.org. Luke is my nephew.

PREFACE

Dave, this book is a collection of stories, observations and some lessons I have learned. I am giving you this book as you graduate from college. I hope this book provokes you to think about everything you experience in life.

According to my friend Espo, some of the stories are not as he remembers them. However, he has said that he likes my versions better.

In addition, I haven't remembered the exact words of the quotations that I have included herein. I have therefore used poetic license throughout the book.

Unfortunately, I didn't start to log these following stories and observations until 2003. So, I have forgotten many stories from Arthur Andersen, Zolfo Cooper and early Policano & Manzo days.

I have asked a couple of guys I used to work with to think about stories I have forgotten. The stories they remembered were more boring than the ones I included, so I didn't include them.

I keep coming up with new observations and remembering old ones. So, I have decided to write a second book. The topics I will cover are listed in the "Coming Attractions" section.

The working title for the second book is "It Is What I Asked For, But Not What I Wanted."

Many thanks to Mark Fogel, my Faux Editor, for his diligence, support and suggestions. Extra special thanks for his wine tips and educational sessions.

Finally, a very special thank you to my cute little wife, Mary. But for her, I would be a controller somewhere instead of living the dream.

OUR FIRST JOB

It was our second day in business at Policano & Manzo, LLC, which was a boutique professional firm that provided financial advisory services to financially troubled companies and their lenders.

The girlfriend of a friend of ours had a friend, who worked for a Savings & Loan in New York. He needed to hire a workout consultant. (You never know where a lead will come from.) So, we put on our suits and headed into New York City.

We met with Stu, a senior lender at the S&L. Stu indicated that the loan in question was the institution's largest loan and that it was for a failed co-op housing project. "So, what do you guys know about co-op housing projects?"

I replied, "One of my friends lives in a co-op."

Stu laughed and said, "No, really, what do you know?"

"Actually, we are not co-op experts or real estate experts. We are troubled company experts. The industry doesn't matter to us."

"Well, it matters to me! I am not going to hire someone on our largest loan that isn't a real estate expert."

I countered, "Listen, a failed co-op conversion is just like a failed LBO (Leveraged Buyout)."

"What are you talking about?"

"Watch, in an LBO, some group with very little money goes to a bank and says, we want to buy this company wholesale and sell off the pieces retail at a high enough price quick enough to pay off the debt and the interest and make some profit."

"The bank says, sure. Get some more money and we will do the deal. The buying group goes around the corner and lines up some mezzanine financing and voila! They buy the company and set off selling the pieces."

"So, the group has to sell the pieces at a high enough price quick enough to pay back the loans with interest and have a profit left over."

"So in a co-op conversion some guy with no money borrows money from you and some other lenders. He buys an apartment building wholesale and has to sell the apartments retail at a high enough price, quick enough to pay off the loans and interest."

Stunned, Stu replied, "It IS like a failed LBO."

"Exactly," I said.

Stu continued, "This is crazy, but I think I will hire you guys. How long have you been in business?"

"Are you looking for an answer in days or hours?"

Stu looking shocked say, "Are you brand new?"

"Well, we started yesterday."

"Would I be your first client?"

"If you hurry."

"I want a discount."

Bob was ready to give him the discount. I jumped in and said, "We can't do that."

"Why not?" Stu asked.

"It wouldn't be fair," I replied.

"Fair to whom?"

"Our other clients."

Stu said, "You don't have any other clients."

I replied, "That is just a timing issue."

He laughed and he hired us. He went on to hire us for four other matters. He then left the bank and went to another bank and hired us there also.

THE HEAD AND THE GUT

When faced with hard decisions, make sure your head (logic) and your gut (intuition) are in the same place.

Every time I have allowed my head to outweigh my gut, I have made a mistake. Your intuition is very strong.

Listen hard, because the head has words and the gut only has feelings. So, if it doesn't feel good, it usually isn't.

COMMUNICATION

It is not possible to over-communicate. Most problems begin, fester and explode because of poor communication.

MY FAVORITE CHURCHILL RETORT

Lady Astor, a member of Parliament and a friend of Churchill's, said when serving tea, "Winston, if you were my husband, I would poison your tea."

Churchill replied, "Lady Astor, if I were your husband, I would drink it".

YOU CAN DO ANYTHING

Invest in yourself. You are your greatest asset.

COMMON SENSE

Common sense is priceless. It just isn't common. Use common sense in everything.

NICHE

Find a niche. Become an expert. Have fun.

CONVENTIONAL WISDOM

Question conventional wisdom. Don't accept it blindly.

WORK THE PROCESS

Do your best and work the process. You can control your effort; you can't control the results.

NUMBER ONE CUSTOMER

Treat your family as your number one customer.

Many people say that their family is more important to them than work. But when a conflict comes up between family and work, I watch people pick work over family time and time again.

But I also observe that when the conflict is another work commitment that they have, they say they have a conflict and can't make it.

So, here is a technique I use. I set my family up as my number one client. I put all my family commitments in my calendar.

When client conflicts arose, I simply tell them that I have a conflict that can't be moved. Occasionally, I wasn't able to meet the family commitment, but I made most of them.

LISTEN

Always listen to what others are saying. Repeat it back to them so you and the speaker know that you understand.

A good listener is always appreciated.

WORRYING

As best as I can tell, worrying never makes anything better, only worse.

TIMELINESS

It is better to be late and right than on time and wrong. (Assuming you can't be on time and right which is always preferable.) Oh, if you can't be on time, let people know.

DO THE RIGHT THING VS. MAKING $$

At the end of the initial work on Donald Trump's restructuring, I was sitting with Joe, Bankers Trust's chief credit officer.

Joe said, "You know, Mike, we never did any work on Donald's three casinos in Atlantic City."

I said, "Yes, I know."

So, he said, "Can you and Pete go down there?"

"Sure. In fact, Pete even has some casino experience. But let me ask you two questions.

If we go down and find out that the three casinos are great properties, are you going to make the loan to Trump?"

"Yes," he replied.

"And if we go down and find out that the three casinos are going to file for bankruptcy in six months. Are you going to make the loan?"

"Yes," he replied. He smiled and asked, "So you are wondering why you have to go?"

"Don't get me wrong Joe. We are a new firm and we can use the fees, but I don't see the need to do this now."

"What do you recommend? he asked.

"Why don't we go down to Atlantic City for a few days after this deal closes and do a quick top down review so that you are aware of the issues."

Joe became a client for life at that moment. He got that I had put his best interest first. This was the type of advice I really enjoyed giving to clients.

INITIATIVE

Develop the judgment to "know when to ask for permission and when to ask for forgiveness."

If in doubt, think of how you would react if you were on the other side. Also, it helps to ask for forgiveness if you have a solid relationship with the other person. If not, err on the side of asking permission.

TRUST

Somewhere along the line, I concluded that people who generally don't trust others, are not trustworthy themselves.

Once I figured this out, it turned out to be true almost all the time.

Also, under stress, one's trustworthiness is often challenged. Be very deliberate when dealing with someone under stress.

THE PRICE

'Cheap' can be very expensive.

SUCCESS

Churchill, "Success is going from failure to failure without losing enthusiasm."

MANAGE EXPECTATIONS

Under-promise and over-deliver.

PROJECTS

They generally take longer and cost more.

(This is especially true for IT projects and anything to do with a house.)

REPUTATION

Warren Buffet once said, "It takes 30 years to build a reputation and 30 seconds to lose it."

BE PROFESSIONAL

Don't curse. It is generally uncalled for and always unprofessional.

CHOICE

From time to time, you will be faced with the choice of telling someone what they want to hear or what you want to say. Choose wisely.

NEVER GUESS A WOMAN'S AGE

Or her weight. Any woman. Trust me on this.

THE STORY

There are always two sides of every story (sometimes more). Don't make any conclusions after hearing only one side no matter how compelling. You will be surprised how compelling the other side of the story is.

EMOTIONS

Stay cool and objective. If emotions get involved, get some help. It is very difficult to be cool, objective and emotional at the same time.

BE A PROBLEM SOLVER

Problem solving is fun. Solving problems is challenging. There is always upside in problems. Seek problems out; solve them.

After you get good at problem solving, people with problems will seek you out.

The key to problem solving is to listen and to understand the problem fully. Also, understand fully what success is, before you start to address the problem.

JUDGING

People will judge you on what you write and what you say. Reread everything you write before you give it to someone.

Speak clearly and concisely, loud enough to grab the attention of the listener but soft enough so you aren't obnoxious.

DO YOUR BEST ALWAYS

Henry Kissinger once had a young man working on his staff. The young man prepared a report and delivered it to Kissinger.

A couple of days later, the young man stopped by Kissinger's office.

"Mr. Kissinger, how did you like my report?"

"Is this the best you can do?" he replied.

The young man took back the report to perform more work. He revised the report the next day.

Again he went to see what Kissinger thought. "How did you like the report?"

Kissinger again asked, "Is this the best you can do?"

The young man took back the report to again try to improve it.

The next day he dropped off the report to Kissinger's office.

Two days later he received a call to see Mr. Kissinger.

"Good morning Mr. Kissinger."

"Young man, is this the best you can do?"

The young man, somewhat annoyed said, "Yes, this is the best I can do."

Kissinger replied, "Good. NOW, I will read it."

GO WITH THE FLOW

As you go through life, some doors will close and you may be disappointed. But other doors you never thought of will open.

RISE ABOVE IT

Stay above the fray of petty issues and complaints of other people.

NOBODY IS PERFECT

Don't expect perfection. Be patient.

SELF-INTEREST

People will usually act in their own self-interest.

THE CEO & INVENTORY

I was at lunch in Dallas with the CEO of a retailer we were working on. The CEO, Dave, asked me what was the major cause of financially troubled companies. I told him that mismanagement was the major cause.

He asked how we evaluate management. And I told him the following.

"Usually, we focus on the management of inventory."

He asked, "What kind of questions do you ask?"

"Well, I ask who is actually in charge of inventory? There usually is someone in charge of buying the inventory, someone in charge of receiving the inventory, someone in charge of storing the inventory, someone in charge of shipping the inventory but, no one is actually in charge of the inventory."

"You know," Dave replied, "no one is in charge of the inventory at my company."

"Yes, I know. That's why I told you this story."

MY GRANDFATHER'S ADVICE

When I was 5 years old, my grandfather told me the following:

Always eat before you go out, even if you are headed to a function that is serving food. You don't know when you will actually eat or if you will like the food.

When I asked what happens if I liked the food, he replied, "You can always eat more."

THE BRIEFCASE THEORY

The amount of 'stuff' that you will take home from work is directly proportional to the size of your briefcase.

THE BRIEFCASE THEORY APPLIED

The lenders to an underwear manufacturer in the Midwest retained us to investigate an inventory problem.

Apparently, the sales force reduced their sales forecast but no one informed Manufacturing. So Manufacturing kept manufacturing underwear.

The problem was discovered by a warehouse manager who called into Corporate and asked where he should put all new inventory.

Apparently, the warehouse was out of room.

AGED INVENTORY

At name-brand women's apparel company in the early '90s, we were looking into the inventory situation. I asked if the company aged its inventory. The finance group said of course they aged the inventory. I asked if I could see a copy of the inventory report.

Sure enough, there were two columns for aging. I asked what they represented and was told, "the left column represents this season's inventory."

"What about the right column?" I asked.

Grudgingly the reply was, "Not this season".

The inventory system only allowed for two columns for aging. Obviously this was not very helpful.

Always ask to see a recent report to verify the answer. It doesn't take much, but it can produce great results.

PLANETARY SYSTEM OF WIP

When we gave the first report on a women's lingerie manufacturer to our clients, the banks, I told them that the Company had a planetary system of work in process inventory.

One of the bankers said, "I never heard of a planetary system of WIP before."

"Neither had I," I replied. "Apparently the Company maintains a list of all work in process.

But they don't keep it by plant, they don't keep it by country, they don't keep it by continent.

They keep it by planet. They know it is on earth. They just don't know where on earth it is."

ARTHUR ANDERSEN GLOBAL BUSINESS CONSULTING GROUP

The best matter I ever worked on was representing the Global Business Consulting Group of Arthur Andersen in 2002.

Like all matters, it was urgent and somewhat out of control. This matter however, was also unprecedented and remarkably complicated.

On the Ides of March, the U.S. Justice Department issued an indictment against Arthur Andersen. The indictment put Arthur Andersen out of business. Andersen was later convicted and then found not guilty on appeal by the Supreme Court.

That same afternoon in March, my buddy Gail, the leader of the Global Business Consulting Group called me. She reached me on the golf course in Hilton Head.

"Mike, the firm has been indicted by the Justice Department. I don't know what to do. You need to help."

I said, "No problem, I would be happy to help. Let me just pull the golf cart up."

Gail replied, "No, not just help. I want to retain you."

We spoke for a few minutes and I said, "fine, I will back on Tuesday." It was Friday.

She said, "No, I am leading a group with $2 billion in revenue, 10,000 people, 175 offices, 85 countries. You must be in NY first thing Monday morning."

So off I went.

WHO DO WE REPRESENT?

I convinced Gail that she needed to hire investment bankers. So, we set out to interview investment bankers including Bear Stearns.

The Co-President of Bear Stearns came to the interview. After a while, he asked, "Whom would we represent? The seller?"

I replied, "No, you wouldn't represent the sellers. They are the legal entities of the various countries that will be part of the proposed sale. They will have their own advisors."

"And no, not the overall partnership. That is a different legal entity which curiously has nothing to sell."

"So, whom would we represent?" he pressed.

I said, "You would represent the assets."

"The assets?" he asked incredulously.

"Yes, what will ultimately be sold will be the people, the assets. So, like us, you would represent the assets."

"I have never represented the assets before. I always represent a buyer or a seller. How will this work?" he asked.

I replied, "I understand. I don't know how this will work but there isn't any other choice."

THE SALE

Aldo from the Paris office replaced Joe from New York as the CEO of Arthur Andersen—Worldwide. (Please use an Inspector Clouseau accent when reading Aldo's part.)

I attended a meeting with Gail and a Bear Stearns gent to explain the proposed sale of Gail's group.

Aldo immediately asked, "Where are the financial statements?"

Gail turned to me and asked me to hand them to Aldo. I gave him a one-page income statement.

The income statement had three lines, revenue, payroll expense and other expenses.

Aldo said, "I don't understand. Where is the detail for the other expenses?"

"Actually, that is all the detail that we have," I replied.

"That can't be possible," he exclaimed.

"I know, I said the same thing."

"Did you ask the CFO?" he asked.

"Yes. She didn't have the information either."

"And this is ok with the buyer?" he asked.

"Yes, we explained that the other expenses were not that important since the potential buyer would be hiring the work force and putting them into their own cost structure. Therefore all they really needed was revenue and payroll numbers."

"Incredible. Let me see the balance sheets."

Again Gail turned to me. I replied, "We don't have any balance sheets."

"What do you mean we have no balance sheets? We are an accounting firm," he stated.

I replied, "Yes, I pointed that out but apparently no one can put together a balance sheet for the group."

"How did you explain this to the buyer?"

"Actually, I thought that was quite magical on our part," I replied.

BREAKING THE TENSION

I was at a meeting at Bear Stearns with my good friends Gail and Mike (outside counsel) regarding the sale of the Arthur Andersen's Global Business Consulting Group. The meeting was getting a little tense.

All of a sudden I said, "excuse me everyone, but isn't Mike's tie pretty weak?"

People started chuckling and pitched in that, yes, Mike's tie was in fact pretty weak. We all laughed. When the meeting broke up shortly thereafter, people were in better spirits than they were a half an hour earlier.

On the way back to Gail's office, I took Gail and Mike a different way.

"Where are we going?" Mike asked.

"I am taking you on the scenic route."

I headed into Brooks Brothers and steered them to the tie shop. I walked up to the salesperson.

"Excuse me. Are you a tie consultant?"

"Yes, can I help you?" he replied.

I turned and pointed to Mike.

"Ah, I see the problem," the tie consultant declared.

Mike, somewhat displeased pointed to my tie. To which, the consultant said, "Very nice."

Gail and I sat down laughing as the tie consultant brought out tie after tie until we found one we liked.

"He will wear it out if it is ok with you."

THE CELL, THE CAB, THE BOX

A week later Gail and I were meeting in New York around midnight waiting for Mike. He finally arrived at the hotel by cab. He sat down, ordered a drink and reached for his cell phone.

Mike said, "Damn, my phone must be in the cab!"

He grabbed my phone and called his phone.

"Hello, yes, you have my phone. Can you bring it back to the hotel now?"

A woman answered, "Listen, it is very late and I am headed home. I work in midtown. Can you pick it up in the morning?"

"Of course," Mike replied.

The next morning I called Mike's cell phone. The woman answered, "Mike?"

"Yes, but not the one you are looking for. I am a friend of Mike's."

"He gets a lot of calls," she said.

"Well, that is because he owes a lot people a lot of money. Can I meet you to pick up his phone?"

She replied, "That would be great. I have answered a lot of calls hoping it was him."

I met the woman a few blocks away. I then went back to Brooks Brothers.

"Excuse, me I need a small Brooks Brothers box and some tissue paper."

I set off to Mike's office in NY. I walked into his office and presented him with the box.

"C'mon, stop trying to dress me," he said.

"Just a little present that I think you will enjoy."

He opened the box. "My phone!!! How did this happen?"

"All part of the full service I provide."

THE FIRST RULE OF HOLES

When you find yourself in a hole, stop digging.

IT'S JUST A FRAUD

Mercury Finance was a large sub-prime auto lender located outside of Chicago. I received a call from the lenders to Mercury saying that the company had announced a fraud and that the lenders wanted to hire us.

Dan and I went to Chicago the next day to meet with the lenders. I was asked what I knew about sub-prime auto lenders. I told the group that I knew nothing about sub-prime auto lenders.

The lead lender indicated that there was an alleged fraud and that we didn't need to spend much time on the business. I replied, "You know you have a broken business here."

The lender replied, "How do you know? You don't know anything about the business."

"True, but I know this. No one commits fraud at a company that is doing well and meeting Wall Streets expectations. One only commits fraud when the company is underperforming."

"Hmmm," the lender replied. "That's an interesting point."

THE CFO IS COMPETENT?

When Ira hired us, I had told him that we would need to rely on his CFO in order to take the job. He indicated that his CFO was up to the task.

Two weeks after we started the job, I asked Ira if I could speak to him. Ira said sure.

"Ira, you lied to me."

"What are you saying? Are you calling me a liar?"

"No, I am not calling you a liar. I just said you lied to me."

"How did I lie to you?"

"You told me that your CFO was competent to do the job and he isn't."

Sheepishly Ira replied, "Yes, I know. But I can't fire him. What should we do?"

"No problem," I replied. "I will get him to resign so that you don't have to fire him."

"How will you do that?" he asked incredulously.

"Actually, it is pretty easy. I am going to ask him to do his job."

"How do you know he will quit?"

"Simple, he will be overwhelmed by what he has to do."

The next day I met with the CFO and set forth all the tasks that had to be performed and which ones he would be responsible for. The meeting took a while since the list was quite extensive.

The following morning Ira called me into his office.

"You're not going to believe this. The CFO resigned this morning. He said he was very sorry but he couldn't handle the pressure of all the issues that needed to be addressed."

"See, I told you it would be easy. Now, how ARE we going to get all this done?"

A COLLATERAL PROBLEM

I was working for the owner of a privately held company. I entered a conference room at the company where some of the outside lawyers and a couple of our guys were working.

"Mike, we are glad you are here. We have a big problem," one of the lawyers said.

"The borrower (our client) pledged the equity of a partnership that owns some land as collateral to two different banks."

"I assume that is somewhat illegal?"

"Highly illegal," they replied.

"How did this happen?"

"Apparently, the land has a mortgage. The equity of the partnership that owned the land had been pledged to one bank a number of years ago.

The company then borrowed from another lender and pledged the equity again but they couldn't find the stock certificates.

There was no record of the initial pledging of the equity. So, the company thought the shares had been misplaced. Outside counsel had new certificates drawn up and they were pledged to the second bank. This is a disaster."

"Well hold on," I replied. "How much is the first mortgage?"

"About $40 million."

"And how much do we think the land is worth?"

"About $20 million."

"Excellent!!!" I exclaimed. "That makes the partnership equity worthless. This is just like the movie "The Producers" with Gene Wilder and Zero Mostel." (This was years before the Broadway play.)

The people in the conference room all said, "What are you talking about?"

"In the movie, the plan was to sell the equity of a new play several times over. Then they would produce an awful play. It would be a flop and close on the first day. The producers would pocket all the money from selling the equity several times after telling each of the other equity owners that the show was a flop."

"The good news here gentlemen, is we have a flop. This means that since the equity is worthless, neither bank is entitled to any recovery from the partnership."

I explained this to the owner who initially was aghast that this had occurred. I then explained it to each of the banks that thought they had the equity of the partnership as collateral. They each understood that their lien if good was, in fact, worthless and neither sued the borrower on that particular matter.

HAVE A SEAT!

A number of years ago, we worked for the banks on an auto parts company owned by a private equity firm. We were meeting with some of the senior company people (but not the CEO) the first day in the boardroom.

Lunch was brought in and set up at one end of the room. About a half hour later, an older gentleman walked in, went to the buffet, picked up lunch and turned to walk out.

"Excuse me," I said.

"You must be important. Because, only an important person would walk into a closed board room with a meeting in process, grab lunch and not say anything."

He laughed and said, "I am the CEO."

"Ah, exactly the person we are looking for. Have a seat and join us."

THE CEO & THE ELEVATOR

I had just started working for the only lender to a small company. I asked to set up a meeting with the CEO who was from Montreal. The word came back that the CEO didn't want to meet with me. In fact, he threatened to quit if he had to meet me.

The meeting did get set up. It was held at Chase Bank on Park Ave. The morning of the meeting, I went up the escalator to the security desk in Chase's lobby.

There was a gentleman just in front of me. I noticed as he was signing in that he was the CEO that I was to meet. I hustled along and stood next to him waiting for the elevator. He had no idea who I was.

I spoke to him and commented that it was a beautiful day. He and I started to chat as we were the only ones in the elevator. We both pressed the button for the same floor.

I kept chatting with him and we got off together. I then wished him a good day.

I went to meet with a couple people from Chase for a few minutes and then went to meet with the CEO and my associate Dave. The CEO still didn't know who I was.

I went into the conference room and introduced myself. We both showed some surprise that we were meeting with each other.

We sat down and I said, "Gee Trevor, you SEEM like a nice guy."

He had a befuddled look on his face.

"I understand that you threatened to quit rather than meet with me. Most people at least wait to meet me before they threaten to quit."

The CEO was at a total loss for words. I told him not to worry. I wasn't going to hold it against him. Our discussion then proceeded on a much better basis for us to extract the information we needed to get.

THE RAVENS

I worked for the lenders to the Baltimore Ravens. The first day I was there, David, the president, stopped by to say hello.

I told him that I wasn't ready to sit down with him and could I speak to him in the afternoon.

Later that day I went looking for his office. The door was open so I looked in. David was on the phone and he motioned for me to come in.

I started walking across his office. He hung up the phone and I stopped halfway across his office.

He said, "What's the matter?"

"Do you have a rest area in here? This office is huge." (There were three different areas with couches and enough sports memorabilia to start a store.)

I continued, "I know how you can solve some of the problem here, sell the practice center and let the team practice here."

He laughed and said, "Screw you."

We got along well after that, but it was a HUGE office.

COMPARISONS OF ACTUAL TO BUDGET

I was working at Arthur Andersen a lifetime ago. I was walking down the hall past the Admin Office and heard some commotion. Inside was my friend, Gary, and an administrator, Lee.

"Hey guys, what's going on? I sense some tension."

Gary said, "Mike come into the office. Lee, what is Mike's status?"

Lee replied, "Mike is one of our stars. He budgeted 40 hours for the week and worked 50 hours. That is a positive 25% positive variance. You, Gary, are a DUD. You budgeted 60 hours and worked 55. That is a 10% negative variance."

Gary was incensed. "But I worked more hours than Mike!! And I made more money for the firm!" Sometimes, Admin, loses sight of the goal.

EAT S**T AND DIE

The Donald Trump negotiations were grinding to a conclusion in the summer of 1990 when the following occurred.

Jim, head of Bankers Trust's real estate group, was having a heated discussion on the phone with Liz, a workout banker from another institution. Donna and Kay, from Bankers Trust, and I were in Jim's office for the call.

The call was marked with numerous expletives deleted and various other verbal barbs. Finally, Jim had lost it and yelled at the phone, "hey Liz, eat s**t and die!" and slammed the phone down.

Donna, Kay and I eased out of the office. Donna said to me, "What are we going to do?"

"I have just the thing, get me a phone book," I replied.

"What are you going to do?" Donna asked.

"I am going to send Liz flowers."

"Flowers???" Donna looked at me like I had three heads. A look, by the way, I was very used to by now.

"Yes, watch."

I dialed the number for a florist in Citicorp Center. "Yes, I would like to send a dozen red roses to Liz Hall on the 40th floor."

"A card? Yes, I would like to send a card. It should say the following, 'eat s**t and die', nothing else."

Donna and Kay who were listening to my side of the phone call cracked up laughing.

Forty-five minutes later, Jim asked us to come into his office. Apparently, Liz was on the line calling in.

Jim picked hit the speaker phone and grunted, "Hello".

At this, Liz starts laughing and says, "I can't believe you did this!"

Jim hit the mute button and asked us what he had done.

I told him that he had sent her a dozen roses with the card, "eat s**t and die."

Jim unmuted the phone and said, "I didn't want you to take it personally."

The negotiations between the two resumed and after the call, Jim said, "That was a good idea I had."

"Yes it was," we replied.

SIMPLICITY

Simplicity is more prized than complexity.

Somehow as businesses grow, things become more complex. Fight complexity at every turn with simplicity. Simplify always!!!

THAT'S GOOD?

Sometimes you don't know what is 'good' until you see what is 'bad'.

BE DUCK-LIKE

Look very calm on the surface and paddle really hard underneath.

CANDOR

Self-confidence is often evident in one's candor.

DON'T ASSUME EXCEPT ...

Assume that everyone hears everything you say, reads everything you write, and sees everything you do.

This will save you a lot of agony over time.

ALSO, ABOUT EMAILS

Assume all your emails are forwarded to others and saved by all. Lesson—don't write anything in emails that you don't want others to see.

WORK THE PROCESS

Dave, did I mention, "Work the process?"

STAY CLOSER TO YOUR ENEMIES

While working on one matter, I ran into Frank, a private bank workout guy from Citibank. At my first meeting with Frank, he was yelling and screaming about the situation.

At the next meeting I brought along counsel for the meeting, Steve and Bob. I told the guys that Frank was a screamer and that my plan of attack was to sit right next to Frank.

Why? It is very hard to yell at someone who is sitting right next to you.

We went into the meeting and I immediately sat down next to Frank, which is highly irregular since the parties usually sit on different sides of the table.

Steve and Bob cracked up as I winked at them.

During the meeting, things got heated and Frank got up to get some water and to yell.

Unbeknownst to him, I had followed right behind him. He turned to yell and was face to face with me.

He muttered, "This whole situation is mind-boggling." To which I replied, "I share your mind-boggledness."

There was no yelling because I was constantly right next to him.

SUPPORT YOUR TEAM

In two weeks on a matter, Bill, one of our new hires, had pissed off every person at Jim's firm, each of the members of our team and, I think, some people he hadn't even met yet.

I brought Bill into my office.

"Bill, I understand that you have pissed off every person here."

"This is how you are going to fix this."

"But Mike, you haven't heard my side of the story."

"Bill, I will stipulate that you have a side of the story, but it is irrelevant. If you want to fix this then you will do what I say."

"But, but, but...."

"No buts. You are going to apologize to every person here. You will tell them it is your fault and that you didn't mean whatever it is you did."

Bill went out to start apologizing.

Minutes later, Jim called me and asked me to go to his office.

I stepped into his office and asked, "So, what's up?"

Jim replied, "We have a problem with Bill."

"Yes, I know Jim. I have spoken to Bill and the problem is being fixed."

"Well, I want Bill taken off the assignment."

"Fine, today will Bill's last day."

"That was easy," replied Jim. "I thought you were going to fight me on this."

"Not at all, Jim. I believe that the client should be able to decide who works on the case. Do you have a piece of paper?"

"Sure, here you go."

I then started writing.

"What are you doing?"

"I am writing the names of my competitors and their phone numbers."

"Why?"

"Oh, didn't I mention that if Bill goes, I go?"

"Hmmmmm, Bill can stay," Jim grudgingly replied.

"Whatever you want Jim."

AL MINTZ STORIES

Al told me he had a lot of good stories. With his permission, I have put them all on this page.

YOU ARE YOUR OWN BUSINESS

Look at your business career as if you are a business.

How do you make yourself unique?

How do you add to your skills and experience?

How do you market yourself?

Who are your customers?

INDUSTRY CONTACTS

When I was at Andersen, I was once told that it would be very helpful to know as many competitors as possible in case I ever need a job.

As I started in the distressed industry, I took this a step further. I figured it made sense to know as many competitors as possible so that when I was on the other side, the competitors would know me. This would initially lend credibility to me and then enable me to be more productive.

COURTESY OF DAN SCOULER

"Never underestimate the power of the negative trend."

C = D + NM

A formula for change is as follows: Change=(very high) Dissatisfaction + a New Model Generally, change occurs when there is major dissatisfaction and a new model. In the absence of either, change is not as likely.

This is especially true as it relates to employees seeking other employment. Employees usually need to be very dissatisfied and have a new job opportunity before they will leave.

This also applies to relationships and other facets of life.

CORPORATE CULTURE

Culture is pervasive in business. Some don't see it and some don't hear it. (One business leader I worked with said, "we don't have a culture").

I think culture is pervasive and deafeningly loud.

Always pick the potential employee that is the better cultural fit. No matter how smart or experienced a candidate is, if he/she is not a good cultural fit, move to another candidate.

I have seen many employers hire employees that had great skills or great experience and then have to let them go a year or so later because they were awful cultural fits.

Be careful to listen to your gut (intuition) here. In each case, the employer admitted to me that they had reservations when they hired the person but explained away those reservations because of the person's skill set.

THIS YEAR/NEXT YEAR

I have worked on hundreds of financially, troubled companies in dozens of industries. And the one constant in each company in talking to management is:

"The current year is always the worst year and next year is always forecasted to be significantly better."

RELATED PARTY ISSUES

Every financially troubled company that is controlled by a family, has related party issues.

(eg., Gitano, Adelphia, Parmalat)

NON-RECURRING WRITE-OFFS

Why do non-recurring write-offs occur every year?

SEMINARS

As soon as you can, start speaking on business topics in front of people. Start at your first job. Then join industry groups. Speak at small gatherings and then at larger gatherings.

As you speak more your name will appear in seminar promotion material sent to industry participants throughout the country. It is a great form of publicity, provides better networking opportunities, you learn more and it adds significantly to your reputation.

WORDS

"We" is usually more powerful than "I".

ON THE OTHER HAND

There were two seconds left in the game when Phil Jackson called timeout. He began to set up the plan to have Pippen shoot the last shot. Michael Jordan said, "I should take the last shot."

Phil replied, "Michael, there is no 'I' in team."

Michael came right back, "Yes, but there is an 'I' in win."

Jordan took and made the last shot to win the game.

GET THE RIGHT TEAM

It is critical to get the right team when dealing with problems.

Two days after Andersen was indicted by the Justice Department, my good friend Gail hired me. She wanted to solve the problem and not 'waste' time getting the right professionals on the team.

On the first day, I advised Gail to hire an attorney. She was adamant that she did not need a separate attorney because Andersen had several law firms. I told her that none of those firms represented her and her group. Each firm represented a different Andersen legal entity. She was unconvinced.

At the end of the first day, there was a conference call with one of the law firms representing the US Andersen partnership. Gail had asked the firm to speak to her partners and answer questions on the situation.

One of her partners asked the attorneys if the partners were incurring additional personal liability every day they stayed at Andersen. Now, bear in mind that Gail was trying to hold everyone in the consulting group together to enable her to sell the whole group.

The attorney replied, "Every day you stay at the firm you are incurring additional personal liability. And we would advise you to leave the firm as soon as possible."

I nearly hit the ceiling. I immediately explained why that was poor advice and not in anyone's best interest.

I then pressed the mute button on the phone and said, "Now can we get our own attorney?"

"Yes," Gail muttered.

DEBT TO SALES RATIO

The first day of Policano & Manzo I sat down to prepare our promotional material. I was debating whether to use the annual revenues or the debt levels of companies we had worked on to indicate the size of the companies.

I discovered that for many of the companies we worked on, the debt levels were about the same as the amount of the annual sales.

I concluded therefore that when total debt is about equal to or greater than the sales of the company, there is a big problem. This has held true so often it isn't funny.

(This doesn't apply to financial companies and certain other companies.)

In early December 2003, I was on the phone with a distressed debt trader in London. We were talking about Parmalat, which was in the paper on a daily basis, but hadn't yet disclosed that it fabricated 4 billion euros of cash.

I said to the trader, "You know, Parmalat is a huge problem."

"What makes you say that?" he asked.

"Look at the debt to sales ratio."

"You mean debt to equity ratio."

"No," I said, "I mean debt to sales."

"I have never heard of debt to sales."

"Yes, I know. It is my own ratio that I have used for over 10 years."

"So what does this have to do with Parmalat?"

I asked him, "What are Parmalat's sales?"

"They are about 8 billion euros."

"And the debt?" I asked.

He yelled across the trading desk for the amount of debt. He got the answer and said, "Holy shit, it is much higher than the sales."

I responded simply, "You need very high margins with that much debt."

MAKE PEOPLE RIGHT

If you first assume that people are right, you can often get to the answer or consensus quicker, even if you think they are wrong.

Use this technique by asking the person how they reached their conclusion. This line of questioning can provide you with insight as to the logic of the other person's position. It also gives you a chance to revisit your own thought process and conclusion.

SOMETIMES PEOPLE ARE NOT GOING TO BE CONVINCED UNLESS THEY CONVINCE THEMSELVES

A number of years ago, I was working on a convoluted real estate credit that had over 50 lenders each with separate lending facilities to a group of related companies. Since it was an out-of-court deal, we needed 100% participation.

With the Agent, we had developed an approach to the situation. However, one person representing a large lender had a different idea.

"Jim's idea can't work," the Agent stated.

"Yes, I know," I replied.

The Agent said, "You have to go convince him that his idea won't work."

"No problem," I replied.

"No problem?? Are you kidding? He is insistent that his idea works!"

"I know. But it doesn't work."

"So how are you going to convince him?" the Agent asked.

"I'm not going to convince him, he is."

"How are you going to do that?"

"Easy, I am going to help him prove his case."

"What are you crazy?" the Agent replied.

"Look," I said. "If I help Jim try to prove his case and he can't prove it with our help, then he will stop pushing his idea and support an approach that works."

"What if his approach works?" the Agent asked.

"Then we will use his approach. But we already know it doesn't work."

Our team spent three or four days working with Jim's team to prove out his approach. Never once did we say it didn't work. After four days, Jim called us in, thanked us for our effort and announced that his approach didn't work.

I reported back to the agent that Jim now supported the Agent's approach. The Agent was stunned that Jim had agreed without any yelling or calls to the Agent.

WORK THE WAY
YOU WANT

One of our first cases was representing Bankers Trust on the Donald Trump matter. Paul, an attorney in BT's legal department had hired us.

Pete and I had started on Monday. On Friday, after spending the week with boxes of information in a windowless room, I went to speak to Paul.

"Hey, Paul, how's it going?"

"Fine, Mike, what's up?"

"Listen Paul, I want to thank you for hiring us in this matter, but this isn't how we work."

"What do you mean?" he asked.

"We work with the principals responsible to resolve problems. All we have done is work with boxes of information. We haven't dealt with the people making the decisions at all. So, I think today will be our last day."

"Wait, let me go upstairs and talk to Joe." (Joe was the chief credit officer of BT.)

Paul returned and said, "Joe would like you to prepare an analysis detailing all the bank claims against Trump, the value of his assets and derive a range of return for the unsecured and undersecured debt. How long will that take?"

"Hang on Paul, let me ask Pete," I replied.

I went to our office and asked Pete to print out the exact analysis that Paul had requested.

I then presented the analysis to Paul.

"How did you know we wanted this?" he asked.

"I didn't know you wanted it, but this is what I would want, so we prepared it."

"Can you stay late to show this to Joe and the team?"

"Sure," I replied.

A little later, I went up to meet with Joe and his team. Joe asked how I knew they wanted this.

"As I told Paul, we just prepared this because this is what I would want to have."

Joe asked if I could come in the next morning, Saturday. I told him I would be there.

The next morning I got there early and prepared another analysis.

Joe and the team came in about 30 minutes later. Joe immediately asked me how long it would take to prepare another schedule.

I turned and handed him the schedule I had just prepared.

"How did you know I wanted this schedule?'

"I figured that this would answer the next question," I replied.

He answered, "I think I am going to like working with you."

We wound up representing all the banks to Donald Trump in the restructuring negotiations for two years thereafter. And we did the work on Trump with one and half people, Pete and I. I know Pete looks like a whole, but he only worked part-time for us at the time.

COMMUNICATION IS KEY

In 1988, the chairman of a creditors' committee of an oil and gas company hired me.

"Bill, thanks very much for hiring us, I will get the paperwork ready to file with the court."

"No Mike. I am hiring you, not the committee. The committee already has retained accountants."

"Why are you hiring me if you already have accountants?" I asked.

"I am hiring you as an interpreter. I want you to tell the committee what the partner of the accounting firm we retained is telling us."

"Why?" I asked.

"We don't understand him. We also want you to tell him what he should be doing because he isn't doing the right things."

MR. SMITH GOES TO NY

I worked on a matter in Oklahoma City or was it Tulsa? Anyway, sometimes the meetings were in Oklahoma and sometimes in NYC.

One time, we were scheduled to have a meeting in NYC. A couple of days before the meeting, it was postponed a week.

On the day of the meeting, I received a call from Mr. Smith, a Big 8 partner. (I am calling him Mr. Smith because that is his name.) He was in NYC and wanted to know where the meeting was. I told him it had been postponed. He had made a long trip for nothing.

Since then, I have confirmed every meeting I have attended before I started traveling.

TELL THEM WHAT YOU HAVE TO SAY

In the mid–80's, I had to testify in Houston to get the firm retained in the bankruptcy of an oil refinery. Lazard was also being retained in the matter. My friend and senior partner of Lazard, David, was testifying for Lazard's retention.

Lazard and my firm, Zolfo Cooper, had been working for the members of the unsecured creditors committee for a few months before the filing and we had both been working for the past two months for the committee even though we hadn't been retained through the Court.

The Company was objecting to our retentions and was represented by a national law firm.

We went to our committee's lawyers' offices the afternoon before the hearing. The lawyers prepped David for a couple of hours. When they finished, everyone started packing up.

"What about me?" I asked.

The lawyer replied, "Don't worry. You saw what we did with David, the questions will be the same."

The next day the Judge called David up to the stand to testify. The attorney asked a number of background questions and then got to the heart of the matter. The questions were awful. David answered them but the questions were not the right questions or in the right order. The Judge was not happy.

David returned to our row and he wasn't happy either. Great I thought. I didn't get prepped. The attorney was asking poor questions. The Judge wasn't happy.

I knew what points I wanted to make. I decided I would make my points no matter what the committee's attorney asked.

The attorney asked me to state my name and address. I did. He asked to me to state the name of my employer. I did. Then I continued on with my monologue. I turned and faced the Judge and explained each of the points I wanted to make. The attorney interrupted me to say he would ask the questions. I kept going. He interrupted again. This time Judge said, "Counselor, Mr. Policano is doing just fine."

Finally, I finished. The Judge was smiling and obviously entertained by this. He asked, "Is there anything else you would like to add before I allow the Company's counsel to cross-examine you?"

"Yes, I do your Honor. I don't understand how the Company's law firm can question my firm's competence to serve in this matter."

"Why is that?" the Judge asked.

"Well, your Honor, our firm currently works with the Company's law firm in seven other matters." I then listed the bankruptcy matters we working on with them.

The Judge then turned to the Company's counsel and said, "Counselors, I think that is a pretty good question. What do you have say about that?"

The Company's counsel stood up. He agreed with the Judge and stated that in light of my testimony they were dropping the objection the ZC's retention.

FN: 20 years later I ran into David on Bond Street in London where we both lived part-time. David is comfortably retired and putting together an annotated bibliography on an English king.

COURTESY OF FOGEL

(Mark not Fred)

THE SOFT TOUCH

Why make a declaration when you can ask a probing question? Having a soft touch gives you flexibility to resolve problems in a cooperative non-threatening manner.

HUMOR AS A TOOL

Humor can be used very effectively to diffuse tension and hostility.

It can be used to reset the agenda mid-meeting.

Humor allows you to float trial balloons. It also enables you to disagree without confrontation.

But, be careful not to overuse, otherwise you risk just being a clown.

FOCUS

Identify the key issues and keep everyone's eyes on them. Don't let issues that appear important but are not key issues cloud your focus.

We were representing the lenders to Xerox who had lent $7 billion unsecured. I was addressing about 200 hundred bankers over a proposed restructuring that gave the banks a $3.5 billion paydown and collateral for the remaining $3.5 billion.

One of the bankers said his institution would not agree to this proposal until the SEC's investigation of Xerox's accounting was completed.

Surely the SEC investigation was an important issue. But it was not a key issue.

I replied to the banker as follows:

You have a choice, you can receive a $3.5 billion paydown and collateral for the remainder of the loan now and not know the outcome of the SEC investigation. Or, you can receive no paydown and no collateral and not now the outcome of the investigation until it is finished whenever that will occur.

By putting the focus back on getting a paydown and collateral, other important issues were exposed as not being key. The focus on the objective clears and clarifies what is really important.

COMMAND OF THE FACTS

Get command of the facts. It is critical to know the company information better than the company (top management).

This is actually easier than you first might imagine. Top management rarely has an intimate knowledge of the numbers. They have a wide range of responsibilities to a number of different stakeholders.

When companies produce numbers, business plans or financial statements, the focus is on getting them done to meet deadlines over getting them right. It is not that management doesn't want to issues right numbers. It is that they don't employ a review process to ensure the correctness. Without the detailed review process, the top management is not intimately familiar with the assumptions underlying the numbers.

If you review the numbers with the people who prepared them, you will often have a better grasp of the facts and the implications thereof than top management.

SEE THE ENTIRE FIELD

Pay attention to all the parties at meetings. Keep one eye on the speaker and one eye on the other participants.

The other participants will give away their thoughts of the speaker's comments with their facial expressions. This technique will put you ahead of the crowd.

Also, consider how stakeholders not at the meeting might react to what is being covered at the meeting.

THE RIGHT ANSWER

When consulting, work the process to get to the right answer. You may disagree with the client or someone senior to you. Remember, you are an advisor, not an advocate.

MAKE IT THEIR IDEA

It is natural to want to get credit for your ideas. But if you are looking to sell an idea, approach the situation by leading the other party to the idea so that they adopt it as their idea. It is the best way to sell your approach.

EGO

Have an incredible sense of yourself and believe you can do anything. Also have an invisible ego.

INCLUSIVENESS

Work hard on listening and observing everyone.

Resist the temptation to think others are not smart. You can learn something from everyone.

This will enable you to believe that everyone is special and then you will treat them as special.

This will also allow you to be inclusive rather than exclusive when addressing problems

EXPERIENCE

You build your experience everyday in everything you do. Experience is a great tool, but don't be a prisoner to your experiences.

There is always another way to do things even if your way works for you.

OPEN MIND

Approach each problem with an open mind. Don't be fooled by preconceived opinions.

That allows you to see nuances.

DEMEANOR

Be ever flexible, ever humble.

THE STICK

Use sparingly, but effectively.

ART OF BEING NON-THREATENING

Be empathetic to others. This will give you more insight into the problem at hand. It will also enable you to address problems in a non-threatening way.

FLEXIBLE AND ADAPTIVE

Don't get wed to an answer. Be flexible and open to new data or new interpretations of data. Work the process.

Too often people identify with an answer and back themselves into a corner. When a better answer presents itself, you must be able move to it with no personal issues.

TIMING

Don't propose a solution until the parties are ready to hear it. I worked on a heated matter in the Midwest where two parties each believed their proposal was the right way to go.

I got on the elevator after one meeting with one of our clients, a banker from Charlotte.

"Mike, you were pretty quiet today."

"Yes,' I replied.

"You need to get an answer for this."

"I have an answer," I replied.

"Well, why don't you tell us?"

"It's too early. The warring parties aren't ready to hear the answer yet. If I tell them the answer now, they will reject it. Then I won't be able to reintroduce the answer for quite a while."

Like a fine wine, serve no answer until people are ready.

Mike Policano

59

BE CREATIVE

Don't be bound by silent boundaries.

When I worked at Zolfo Cooper, I was assigned to work on a Chapter 7 liquidation in the Bronx. However, the company no longer had any employees, just boxes of information.

After spending the afternoon in the warehouse with the boxes, I decided this was not the best use of my time. But, I was responsible for the work.

I decided to call my friend Nancy. Nancy was just starting her own accounting firm. I asked her if she was interested in doing the work I was doing. She agreed.

The next morning I went into the office to speak to Frank.

Frank asked, "What are you doing here?"

"Frank, have I got an idea for you. We can hire my friend Nancy as a subcontractor to do the work that I will oversee. Nancy gets some work, we can charge the estate less and I will be free to do other work."

Frank replied, "That IS a good idea. Make it happen."

AS A WORKER

Spend your energy on large efforts not on small annoyances.

EXCELLENCE

Require excellence and meaningful contribution from everyone. People resent it when others are not held to the same standards.

COMPENSATION

No matter how much we are paid, we want to be respected and thanked.

EFFECTIVE LEADERSHIP

Peter Drucker said to be an effective leader, you must recognize that the business you're really in is the obstacle identification and removal business.

EXPENSES AND THE HAT

Back in the old days of the accounting profession, the staff and partners were required to wear business hats to work.

One young staff guy put his hat on his time report to be reimbursed by Arthur Andersen. The firm denied the expense. The staff person argued that he only wore the hat for work so the firm should pay.

The next month the staff person put his hat on his expense report again. It was rejected again.

Two months later, the staff person went on an extended business trip. When he handed in his time report, he included a note that said, 'find the hat now.'

LEADERSHIP

It is all about leadership in every organization.

Leaders think then act.

Leaders are responsible and accountable.

Leaders are rational yet intuitive.

Leaders have a vision that is communicated to employees, customers and all stakeholders.

Leaders bring out the best in people.

Leaders have initiative.

Leaders see the broader picture.

Leaders help others.

Leaders have common sense.

Leaders are excellent communicators.

Leaders listen.

Leaders value doing the right thing.

Leaders trust others and are trustworthy.

Leaders are problem solvers.

Leaders support their teams.

Leaders say "we" not "I".

Leaders give credit and take blame.

Leaders know it is about the questions, not the answers.

Leaders are logical.

Leaders look to simplify.

Leaders have followers that want to make the

Leaders proud of them.

STRATEGY

Not too long ago, it occurred to me that developing a corporate strategy is just like planning a vacation.

So I started to ask CEO's I worked with to answer the vacation questions when explaining their corporate strategy.

They would always say, "What does that mean?"

I would reply, "What is the first question you have to ask and answer before you plan your vacation?"

They would invariably answer, "Where do I want to go?"

"Excellent, now we can begin the discussion."

I would then lead them into the follow-up questions. When are you going there? How are you going to get there? How much time do you have or need? How much will it cost? Have you told your employees?

The last question usually was met with a 'not really'.

I would reply, "So imagine if you told the family you were all going on vacation, but didn't tell them where you were going."

Some would pack for warm weather, some for cold weather and some not at all.

YOUR STRATEGY

From time to time, ask yourself the vacation questions. Oh, answer the questions also.

SOME SELLING ITEMS

WHAT ARE WE SELLING?

When we set up the Policano & Manzo, we defined the service we were selling as 'solving the client's problem', both the company's problem and the individual's problem.

We provided a leadership service vs. a support service. This was a value-added service vs. a commodity service.

We were a confidant and trusted advisor to the CEO or the agent bank as appropriate.

SELL TO THE CEO

We sold to the CEO. Our competitors sold to the CFO. Selling to the CEO had several benefits.

First, this problem is one of the biggest problems of the CEO's life. The CEO hasn't been through this process before and there is fear and uncertainty that the CEO can't show because, well, he or she is the CEO.

Second, advising the CEO in an empathetic manner allows one to make the most impact.

Third, working closely with the CEO ensures the highest probability of collecting all of the fees. The CEO knows exactly what you have done and understands the benefit. If you work directly for the CFO, the CEO has no idea what the firm is doing. Moreover, the CFO can blame the firm in private for mistakes that may be the CFO's fault.

Fourth, the CEO makes the best reference for other matters.

QUESTION CONVENTIONAL WISDOM

All of our competitors put together large pitch books when seeking new assignments.

These firms would spend many hours and dollars to assemble these books. The books generally stated all the services they provided, included recent historical financial statements and some small piece on the current situation.

I concluded that these pitch books were not necessary to win new assignments. In my view, the books took too much time to put together and that reduced chargeable hours, the production costs were high, they were usual done under intense time pressure and they were not fun for the staff doing the work.

We put out a simple statement of qualifications that listed the key assignments we had worked on and the people we had worked with from various institutions.

It was very rewarding to see potential clients immediately go to the cases we worked on and list of industry players. It gave us instant credibility.

We then put together a one or two page issues list in bullet points.

This was a fabulous technique. Watch how it worked at Kmart. The Financial Institutions Committee interviewed us. We presented two pages of potential issues. They were essentially discussion points for which we had no answers.

We were retained by the Committee an hour after the interview and started immediately.

The Chairperson asked counsel how the Committee should proceed. He replied, let's start with the Policano & Manzo issues list. It appears to touch on almost every item this group needs to address.

LEVERAGE IN SALES NEGOTIATION

Leverage in a sales negotiation is highly dependant on your ability to walk away without the sale or the purchase.

If you can walk away without getting the sale, then you have the strength to negotiate hard.

If you aren't able to walk away, the other side will smell the weakness and take advantage of you.

SHORT TERM THINKING

The management of publicly held businesses is under tremendous pressure to employ short-term thinking often to the detriment of the long-term health of the business.

LOGICAL?

Always look for the logical reason when something or someone looks illogical.

If it looks illogical, there is usually a problem. And behind the problem is generally a performance or compensation issue.

SMART???

Some people think that explaining something in a complicated matter shows how smart they are.

I always found it was much better to dissect a complicated situation into small, discreet pieces to analyze and then present.

Simplifying an explanation so that everyone can understand it is the smarter way to go.

INDEPENDENT THINKING

Thinking differently than everyone else is an asset. Don't be afraid to question what others readily accept.

One of my favorite questions, even today, when someone makes a statement is "what does that mean?"

REPORTS

Frequently, the best way to report on something is to report in chronological order. It demonstrates the thought process based on what was known when.

HUMAN NATURE

Observe human nature always. It will give you great insight as to whether to accept what is being presented to you.

SKEPTICISM

Healthy skepticism should be employed liberally in all matters.

BE OPEN TO NEW DATA

I had a client named Tom who was very bright and outspoken. At one meeting, he proclaimed the approach that he believed the group should take.

I asked, "Tom, if I told you the following facts (I ticked off half a dozen facts) what would you say?"

"Are they all true?" he asked.

"Yes." I replied.

Tom answered, "Then, I disagree with everything I just said."

JUST AN ACCOUNTANT

The financial advisor for Trump in his restructuring was a partner of an international accounting firm. He had a habit of saying "I am just an accountant" when addressing the lenders.

One day Pete and I had a meeting at Trump Tower with this partner and two of his partners. At the end of the meeting, I said, "by the way don't keep saying 'I am just an accountant'; be proud of it."

As we were walking down the hall, Pete said, 'I can't believe you said that. Do you know who he is?"

"Sure, why?"

"Mike, he is the managing partner of the firm."

I replied, "Really? Then he definitely shouldn't say he is just an accountant."

VALUATION

We were working for Al, a venture capitalist with significant investments in three dozen companies. I asked Dave, one of our guys, to meet with Al and ask him what he believed his equity in the investments was worth.

Dave told me that Al said his equity was worth $800 million. I immediately went to see Al.

"Hey Al, you are a very funny guy."

"What do you mean?" Al asked.

"You know, that joke you played on Dave; $800 million of equity. That's pretty funny."

Al was not amused. "What do you mean a joke? You don't think the equity is $800 mil?"

"I KNOW it is not worth $800 mil," I replied.

"What do YOU think it is worth?" he said.

"I don't know what the equity is worth. But I KNOW your equity is not worth $800 million," I replied.

"Why do you KNOW the equity is not worth $800 million?" a very annoyed Al asked.

"Well Al, you are a pretty smart guy right? After all, although you have 36 people working for you, it really is all about you. How much do you owe the banks?"

"Around $400 million."

"So, why would a smart guy like you hire a guy like me, when you have $800 million of value to spread over $400 million of debt?"

"Hmmm, you have a point" Al mused. "So what do you think?"

"Has to be worth only $200 million. That's the point at which you would ask for help."

POLITICS

I was in Baltimore for an Orioles game in the team owner's box. The owner asked me to meet someone. "Mike, this is Bill Cohen."

"Hi Bill, how are you doing?"

"Fine" he replied.

"So, Bill, what do you do for a living?"

He laughed, "I am one of the two US Senators from Maine."

"Oh. Well, how do you like that job?"

Bill and the owner just bust up laughing.

Bill said, "No one ever asked me that before."

Bill's next job was Secretary of Defense of President Clinton. I wonder how he liked that job?

A BRIEFCASE STORY

One day Tom, a client, stopped me to ask a question. "Hey Mike, why is it that every time I see you, you have a thin briefcase and one of your other partners has a big overloaded briefcase?"

"That's because he is Italian." I replied.

Tom said, "But, YOU are Italian."

I replied, "No, I am a fake Italian. He is a real Italian."

"So, why does the real Italian need a bigger briefcase?" he asked.

"Because, real Italians carry grudges."

DINNER ANYONE?

In the third week on the Trump matter, we were working late. Joe, Bankers Trust Chief Credit Officer, asked around 1am if anyone wanted to go to dinner.

I said I was staying at a hotel and that I would have dinner with him. So the two of us went over to Christo's for a light dinner of steaks and beer.

"So, Mike, I never heard of you guys before. Do you do much work for Bankers Trust?"

"Actually Joe, this is our first matter with BT."

"Really? How many people are in your firm?"

"Two and a half," I replied.

"A half?"

"Yes, I know Pete looks like at least a whole, but he only works part-time for us."

"Mike, take this the right way, but this is a pretty high profile matter. Why did we hire you?"

I took a swig of beer and replied, "Joe, take this the right way, I don't know. But I figure now isn't a good time to ask."

He laughed and asked, "How long has your firm been around?"

"Two months." And then I told him our story.

He asked if we had any money.

"None that I am aware of," I replied.

For the next six months, Joe had me hand deliver our invoice to him each month and he wrote out a check right then and there while I waited.

A ROBBERY?

My very first bankruptcy matter was a New Jersey convenience store chain, Garden State Farms. Amongst my duties was to determine how much cash the company had and to reconcile the bank accounts.

As I checked the company's bank reconciliations, I kept noticing a reconciling item called "RIT".

I finally asked the treasurer what was an "RIT"?

She replied, "That is a robbery in transit."

I said, "I am sorry, I am pretty new at this. What is a robbery in transit?"

She replied, "Well, we record revenues for each of our stores based on the nightly cash deposit. Sometimes, the clerks get robbed on their way to deposit the money in the bank.

We have to record an entry for "robbery in transit" to make sure our revenues are right."

"But doesn't that overstate cash?" I asked.

"Yes, but it is supposed to be adjusted downward by the accounting department."

Unfortunately, accounting forgot to adjust the cash balance down. Oh well.

A CHRISTMAS NOTE

I once sent a Christmas note to a bank client listing some of the statements the company and its advisors made to us during the previous six months. A number of these statements come under the 'you had to be there' heading.

For better or worse, these are all true.

Players: The advisors are all investment bankers hired to represent the Company.

ADVISOR—"The company doesn't have the means to prepare a weekly cash flow forecast. Moreover, we don't think it is a reasonable request."

CFO—"I wasn't able to do the analysis. My dog died."

ADVISOR—"He is the best CFO I have ever dealt with."

ADVISOR PARTNER—"You are aware that the receivable financing expires in three days and no one is negotiating with the financing company."

ADVISOR ASSISTANT—"We believe in the numbers." The company ran out of cash three weeks later.

ADVISOR—"I didn't look at the numbers in detail."

CFO—"By the way, Peat Marwick will be issuing a *qualified* opinion. Is that a problem?"

ADVISOR—"Assistant, whose interest is this in the forecast?"

ADVISOR—"I haven't read the whole financing agreement yet. I will send it to you when I am done." Two days later, we received the entire agreement, both pages.

ADVISOR ASST—"Advisor, it is the banks' interest."

ADVISOR PARTNER—"Actually, I haven't spoken to the CFO in three months."

ADVISOR—"The Governor of New York will be calling the bank's CEO in the morning."

ADVISOR—"Assistant, are we paying the bank' interest?"

TAX PARTNER—Gave a brief explanation of the revised new tax story for the owner and the company using the following words, "amend, offset, reimburse, net, retain, remit, submit, file, re-file, re-amend, etc."

ADVISOR—"I don't know how the $1.1 million is calculated. Somebody told me. I don't remember who."

CRISIS MANAGER—"Our options are like those of the princess bride. The story goes as follows.…"

LIMO DRIVER—"I drove one of your bank participants home last night. When I asked him for directions, he replied, 'I don't know how to get home by car. I have only lived there three months."

URGENT

When everything is URGENT, nothing is urgent.

15 MINUTES IN BALTIMORE

I was working for Jim at the time. We had a large meeting with his bank lenders. One of his largest lenders walked out of the meeting midway.

The next day I called Don, the lender who left the meeting early. I asked if I could come down to Baltimore to meet with him. He said, no. I tried again to get him to agree to meet and again he said, no.

Finally, I said, "Can I just have 15 minutes?"

"Just 15 minutes? You would come all the way down just for 15 minutes?"

"Yes."

The next week I took Amtrak down to Baltimore and met with Don on Monday morning.

"Good morning Don."

"Good morning Mike. As I said, only 15 minutes."

"No problem," I replied.

I walked into his office and noticed an interesting painting on his wall.

"Is this the Baltimore harbor?"

"Yes."

"What year is this?"

"1884"

"A local artist?"

"Yes."

"Where would the current harbor be?"

"Mike, you have less than 10 minutes left. Are you just going to talk about the painting?"

"Well, Don, I might as well. I can't cover anything substantive in 15 minutes."

He laughed and said, "OK, what do you want to discuss?"

I spent three hours in Don's office including lunch.

PROBLEMS AND CHALLENGES

In life, you trade off one set up problems for another. Pick the set of problems you want to deal with.

EMBRACE THE SHIELD

A couple of years ago out of 100 caddies at the club, I had The Shield as my caddy eight out of nine times. The Shield just grated on me.

He commented on each of my shots. This would have been fine if any of my shots were good or if he commented to himself. Furthermore, the next lost ball the Shield finds will be the first.

But, I couldn't complain about The Shield or ask for another caddy. I didn't want to jeopardize his job. And I couldn't change his behavior.

So, I changed my attitude towards The Shield. Of course, I had The Shield as my caddy the next time out. This time I yelled to him, "Shield, it is good to have you again. I went on the offensive commenting on everything to The Shield. I had a wonderful time.

That was two years ago and I haven't had The Shield since.

YANKEE TICKETS

In April 1994, I received a call from Al that the Yankees tickets we have were available for sale. I had to decide on the call whether we wanted them. I said 'yes'.

I hung up and wondered, how was I going to unload 420 tickets? Seventy games, six tickets a game.

I started to call around but found no takers. The Yankees were pretty awful at the time. I called Richard who had a law firm.

Richard replied, "We are Mets fans."

"I won't hold that against you. Just try one game."

He went to one game and said he would buy half the tickets, 35 games.

Two years later, the Yankees were playing well and went to the World Series. We had a great time. Then the next March, I received a call from Al. The owner of the tickets wanted half the tickets since the Yankees were now good.

I called Richard, "Richard, bad news. The owner of the tickets wants half the tickets."

Richard replied, "That is bad."

"Actually it is worse for you."

"Why is that?" he asked.

"He wants your half."

PROBABILITIES

I was working for Ted, an individual who controlled several companies that had borrowed over $500 million that he couldn't pay back.

Ted asked, "What is the probability that I will stay out of bankruptcy?"

I replied, "5%".

"That low?" he asked.

"Actually, it is lower. I rounded to the nearest 5%."

DON'T SKIP VACATIONS

There is always a work reason for skipping a vacation. If you skip it, you will always remember missing the vacation, you will never remember why.

BUCONERO

Be very careful what you name projects. A name may seem funny or clever when created. But if there is ever a problem, the name may not seem so funny or clever.

A Citibank banker working with Parmalat, Ltd., named a lending facility 'Buconero'. Parmalat Ltd., was an Italian company that was accused of a massive fraud.

What does 'Buconero' mean in English? Black Hole. In hindsight, perhaps that was not the best choice.

SPEAKING OF OTHERS

Never speak negatively of others. You don't know who will say what to whom and others may wonder what you say about them when they are not there.

204 ½ Brick Street

Steve and I went to Philly for a meeting on a new situation. The address was 204 ½ Brick Street behind the Liberty Bell. We walked up and down the street but couldn't find the address.

Finally, I said, "Steve, just look for a parking area with expensive cars. People who owe a lot of money always have expensive cars."

Shortly afterwards, Steve said, "Look here. A Mercedes 500SL, a Dodge Viper and a Jaguar."

"This is it," I said. Steve replied, "But Mike, it might not be the right office."

We walked into the unmarked building. I walked up to the receptionist and said, "We are here to see Frank Stevens."

"Yes sir" she replied, "Who should I say is calling?"

WHO ARE THESE GUYS?

(courtesy of Dan Scouler)

Dan was working for a company in Seattle. The company filed for Chapter 11 protection in Delaware. The company hired a local attorney from Seattle. The attorney asked the CEO, who are these financial advisors you hired? I never heard of them.

There had been a couple of hearings in the Delaware court and many people seemed to know Dan and Policano & Manzo. Bob, from our firm, attended one of the court hearings in Delaware. He was walking down the hall and ran into six or seven different people he knew.

The Seattle attorney commented that we knew a lot of people for someone he never heard of.

The Delaware judge was under pressure to transfer the case to Seattle and she did. The Seattle attorney was very happy. Now they were going back to his territory and he would be in charge. Not P&M, who he didn't know.

The judge in Seattle called for a conference with the various parties so that she could get up to speed on the case.

The group met in the Judge's chambers. The Seattle attorney introduced the parties to the judge.

When he got to Dan, he said, "This is Dan Scouler with Policano & Manzo. His firm …"

The judge interrupted the attorney, "I know of Policano & Manzo counselor. Good morning, Dan. How are Mike and Bob?"

YOU AREN'T FUN

We were representing a bank group that had a $300 million loan to a company that was owned by a private equity firm. We were meeting with representatives of the private equity firm to discuss the range of valuations of various subsidiaries of the company.

Don and Jim were the two private equity guys. They were joined by Dennis, their outside consultant, John, an outside director and Bill, their attorney.

Don and I were discussing the state of affairs and he was, how shall I say, getting agitated.

Don started raising his voice and cursing. I continued to answer back to him in a calm voice. He kept yelling and swearing.

All of a sudden, I turned to Dan Scouler of our firm and asked,

"Dan, are you having fun?"

Dan laughed and said "No."

I replied, "Neither am I."

I turned to our counsel and asked, "Arthur, are you having fun?" He was too stunned to answer.

I turned back to Don and said, "You aren't fun. So I am not going to speak to you anymore. I stood up and moved my chair sideways so that I was looking directly at the rest of Don's team and looking away from Don.

I addressed the rest of the private equity team and said, "You guys look like fun. I will speak to YOU."

Don started to speak and I raised my hand towards him. Without looking at him I said, "I am not speaking with you."

The discussions continued with Jim and his team for another 30 minutes. At the end, I asked, "Who should I get back to after I speak to the Banks?"

Jim replied, "You can get back to Don or me."

I said, "Obviously, I will get back to you. Don isn't fun."

Everybody (except Don) chuckled as the meeting broke up.

The next day I received a call from John, the outside director.

John said, "I can't believe you did that yesterday. That was great. It was my first meeting with Don and Jim. I can't believe Don's behavior."

I replied, "John, life is too short to deal with people like Don."

THE PUTZ

I was having breakfast with my long-time friend, Joan. Joan is a nationally recognized high school volleyball and softball coach.

Joan was commenting that her new principal had upset her. Apparently, he had come down very hard on some students for their participation in an activity led by Joan.

Joan was determined to meet with the principal on Monday and let him know that his methods were not appropriate for the given situation.

So I asked Joan, "What do you expect to happen at this meeting?"

She replied, "I expect him to see the error of his ways."

"Not going to happen," I stated.

"Why not?" she asked.

"Because, the guy is a Putz."

"How do you know that?" she asked.

"I can tell by your story. He is a Putz. Only a Putz would have done what he did. Now here is the problem in dealing with a Putz. For the Putz, it is all about the Putz. It isn't about doing the right thing. It isn't about the school or the students. It is all about the Putz.

The Putz must look good at all times. The Putz cannot admit the he or she did something wrong.

So, your meeting with the Putz will turn out to be about what you did wrong, because the Putz is always right."

She went to the meeting with a new agenda. I received a message from Joan after the meeting. She indicated that she just listened. She did mention one thing the principal could do better. The principal disagreed. She said she almost laughed sitting there listening to him, the Putz.

ANOTHER PUTZ

Another long-time friend, Diane, is a dedicated special-education teacher. She had told me a story about her new school principal.

Apparently, someone had come up with the idea that special-ed students should be taught in the same classroom as regular students, at the same time, by a different teacher.

Diane had to teach seven students in a class of 33 students at the same time as the regular teacher in the same room. So Diane used her common sense and led her students into the hall and used a table to gather her students and teach.

However, the new principal saw this and told Diane, that she was required to be in the classroom. Obviously, this was silly.

This story reminded me of the following:

A PUTZ favors bureaucracy over common sense.

CREDIBILITY

Credibility in business and in life is huge.

You build credibility by doing what you said you would do when you said you would do it.

Integrity is a requirement to have credibility.

BREAKDOWNS

Breakdowns provide opportunity for breakthroughs.

SILENCE

People have a hard time with silence in interviews and negotiations.

A few well-placed moments of silence can be exceedingly rewarding.

FREDDIE AND HIS HAIR

I landed around 11pm in Boston one night. In the cab on the way to the hotel, I got a message from Freddie who was advising the company on a West Coast matter I was working on with the banks. Freddie wanted me to call him ASAP.

When I got to the hotel, I called Matt from our firm and dialed in Freddie. Freddie started yelling about what my clients were doing.

I don't like getting yelled at, especially at midnight and especially by Freddie who is 10 years older than me and has no grey hair.

As Freddie was yelling, I said, "Freddie stop a second. Freddie, stop! I have an important question."

"What is it?" he replied.

I said, "You're 10 years older than me right?"

He replied, "Yes, so what?"

"And you have no grey hair, right?" I continued.

"That's right," he said.

I replied, "So, tell me the truth. Do you dye your hair?"

Matt roared laughing. Freddie protested that he didn't dye his hair.

I replied, "Come on Freddie, we are friends, I won't tell anyone."

Freddie said, "Absolutely not!"

"Freddie, come on"

The steam was taken out of Freddie's sails and the yelling stopped.

PAINTED IN A CORNER

In 1987, I was working for the bank group in the LTV matter. The group had co-heads, Steve and Ed. Steve was the head of a large bank workout group in the US.

One day Steve called me and asked me to set up a meeting with him, the CFO of LTV and me.

I replied, "No problem. I will give Ed a call and see when he can make it."

Steve growled, "I don't want Ed at the meeting. And I don't want you to tell him. Do you understand?"

"Sure, no problem" I replied. "Steve, how would you feel if Ed calls me next week and asks me set up a meeting with the CEO without you?"

Steve yelled, "Alright, invite him!"

I replied, "Whatever you want Steve."

THE REVIEW

I have noticed that people are often reluctant to take constructive advice in work matters. In fact, people are often defensive in these situations.

I was giving Bill a review on a matter we worked on. I was explaining how he could do some things differently on the next matter.

He was sitting in my office with his arms folded, a sure sign that he wasn't happy with this conversation.

"Bill, you don't look happy about this discussion," I commented.

He replied, "No, I am not happy at all."

"That's pretty funny," I said.

He said, "I don't think it is funny."

"I think you will find it funny when I explain. We play a lot of golf together, right?"

Bill replied, "Yes, we play a lot of golf."

"And I am pretty bad right?" I asked.

"Yes," he laughed. "You are pretty bad."

I then said, "So, even though I am a lousy golfer, when I make suggestions to you regarding golf, you happily accept them, right?"

"Right," said Bill.

I continued, "Now, I am an expert at our work, yet when I make suggestions, you shut down and don't listen. Isn't that funny?"

Bill laughed and said, "Well, when you say it that way, it is pretty funny."

DO YOU HAVE ID?

It was a Monday morning in February. Frank, Len and I were traveling to Chicago for a series of meetings on Continental Illinois National Bank (CINB).

At the end of the day, Len and I joined Mike from CINB for dinner and Frank went to dinner with Mark from CINB.

The next morning Len and I were scheduled to meet Frank for breakfast at 8 am. By 8:15 Frank hadn't showed up. So I called the hotel operator and asked to be connected to his room. The operator indicated that there was no Frank staying at the hotel.

I called Mark to confirm that he dropped Frank off at the right hotel after dinner. Mark confirmed that he had dropped Frank at our hotel at midnight.

I then called Frank's secretary in New York. She indicated that she had not heard from Frank.

So, Len and I had breakfast and waited to hear from Frank. At 10:30, the phone in my room rang. It was Frank.

Frank growled, "Meet me in the lobby."

Len and I met Frank in the lobby. Frank looked like a mess. He was unshaven, unkempt and tired. Frank stomped over to the front desk and demanded to see the manager.

The manager came out to speak to Frank. "Yes, can I help you sir?" he asked.

Frank, while smoking, venomously spit out the following story.

"Let me tell you what happened to me last night. I arrived here last night at midnight. I went to the front desk to check-in."

"Good evening, I am checking in," Frank said to the clerk at the front desk.

The clerk replied, "Good evening sir, your name please."

Frank gave her his name.

"Ah yes, here you are sir," she replied. "How will you be settling your account?"

Frank replied, "I will be paying in cash."

"Cash sir?"

"Yes, cash," Frank replied. "I was skiing yesterday in Vermont and I lost my wallet. Is cash a problem?"

"No sir. Cash is fine. Do you have any form of identification?"

Frank replied, "As I said, I lost my wallet yesterday and my ID was in my wallet."

"I see sir," the clerk replied. "Please wait a moment sir."

A couple of minutes later the night manager came out from the back. "Sir, I understand that you are settling your account in cash and you have no ID."

"Yes, I lost my wallet in Vermont yesterday."

She replied, "Sir, if you have no ID, you can't stay here."

"Miss, I have a thousand dollars. Take it and in the morning give me back what you don't need."

"Sir, please, you have no ID you can't stay here"

Frank pleaded, "Wait, two of my guys are staying here."

She checked the computer and said, "Yes, I see they are checked in."

Frank said, "They can ID me!"

The manager said, "Sir, I will be right back." She returned with two security guards. "Sir, I am sure you don't want to make a scene. These men will escort you out of the hotel."

Frank asked, "Can I call my two guys?"

"Yes," she replied, "But not from here."

Frank was escorted out of the hotel. If Frank had turned left, he would have gone down Magnificent Mile which has several upscale hotels. But Frank chose poorly. He turned right.

Frank then told the day manager that he stayed at a hotel that only took cash and he had to share a common bathroom.

I then butted in and said, "Sir, we back at the office would find it particularly humorous if you were to inform Frank that technically he was a no-show last night. And accordingly, he was probably charged for last night."

The day manager laughed and said, "You know, you are right, he probably was charged."

Frank erupted. "I want the night manager fired! This is outrageous!"

Frank was obviously fit to be tied. I decided not to tell him that I had been upgraded and had a junior suite with two beds and two bathrooms.

KMART'S CEO

We were advising the Financial Institutions Committee in the Kmart bankruptcy in 2002.

I arrived late for a meeting with the professionals for the Kmart and the Committee. I sat next to John, one of our guys. An attorney for Kmart was summarizing the proposed employment contract for the CEO.

As I listened, I wrote down the financial terms of the proposal that covered a successful scenario and a severance scenario.

As I added the amounts, I noted an odd outcome. I asked John if I had the right amounts. He confirmed that I had the right amounts.

I interrupted the meeting. "Excuse me. I am sorry I was late. Can I just summarize my understanding of the contract proposal?"

"Let me list the amounts that the counsel for Kmart has laid out." I listed the amounts due to the CEO if he led a successful emergence from bankruptcy and said, "I don't have a calculator but is that roughly $12 million?"

An attorney for the company said, "Yes, it is approximately $12 million."

"Thank you," I said. "Now let me list the amounts due to the CEO if he is terminated after one year."

I listed the amounts and said, "Is that around $16 million?"

Someone replied, "Yes, it is $16 million."

To this I asked, "Am I the only one here who thinks it is odd that if the CEO is fired, he gets $16 million which is more than the $12 million he gets if he is successful?"

THE $30 MILLION COMPANY

My buddy Roger, from a money center bank, called me with a new matter.

"Mike, I have a small matter that I would like you to help me with. It is only a $30,000,000 company."

"No problem," I said. "How much is the debt?"

"About $35 million," Roger replied.

"And where is the company located," I asked.

Roger answered, "The CEO is located in Montreal, the CFO is located in New York, there is an accounting office in Hong Kong and there are manufacturing facilities in Brooklyn, Secaucus, Alabama, Mexico and Philippines."

I laughed, "Roger, let me save you some money. This is the World's Largest $30 million Company. It can't repay $35 million in debt."

MAKE IT PERSONAL

I recently met with the accounting group of a company. The accountants commented on the lack of response they were receiving from the rest of the company.

Jill complained, "They don't respond to us. And we can't get our work done."

Cathy said, "I think they don't respond on purpose. I think it is personal!"

I responded, "I am in a somewhat unique position. I was an accountant, I had my own firm and I was a professional supported by accounting departments. People are not purposefully ignoring you. People are just responding to the hottest fire of the day. Trust me, it is not personal at all."

"In fact, to fix this situation you must make it personal! A personal relationship with others will greatly increase their response to you."

LUGGAGE

In 1999 I was working for a bank group in a matter in San Jose, CA. The night before a meeting with the company, I stayed at a hotel across the street with two bankers.

The next morning we met for breakfast and then headed out to the meeting. As we walked out of the hotel, Julie and Jill, the bankers, asked me:

"Why do you have your luggage with you?"

I replied, "A good workout guy never gets separated his luggage."

Jill laughed, "But Mike, the meeting is right across the street. We can get our luggage after the meeting."

I replied, "That is the plan now. The plan may change, time might get tight."

They just laughed.

The meeting ran late that day. We were late to leave for a meeting in San Francisco. We ran across the street to get Jill and Julie's luggage. Of course, it took a long time to get their luggage from the valet. I just smiled.

Two weeks later, I was at a meeting in Florida. One of the bankers, Bill, decided to leave early to fly to Chicago.

Thirty minutes later, Peter another banker, groaned, "Oh no!"

"What is it?" I asked.

Peter replied, "I left my luggage in Bill's car. And he is headed to Ft. Lauderdale airport and I am going to West Palm Beach airport."

This is why a good workout guy never gets separated from his luggage.

Do you know where your luggage is?

TRAVEL FOR FUN

A few years ago I drove to TPC Boston to play golf with Mark and Rich. Part way through the round Rich asked me the following:

"Mike, what are you doing up here in Boston anyway?"

"I am here to play golf with you two," I replied.

Rich said, "That is crazy! You drove here just to play golf with us?"

"Crazy?" I asked. "If I came here for a meeting, would that be crazy?"

Rich replied, "No that wouldn't be crazy."

I then said, "Ok, what would you prefer to do, go to a meeting or play golf?"

"Play golf of course," Rich replied.

"So why is driving here for a meeting 'ok' and but driving here for golf is crazy?"

"I didn't look at it that way," he replied.

"Well, I do. I will travel as far for fun as I would for work."

POLICANO & MANZO

"Conventional Wisdom Turned on its Head"

"Better" is usually unique, however, "unique" is not always better.

VISION

We had a vision for P&M that was unique in the marketplace in 1990. P&M was a specialized boutique of experienced professionals advising senior lenders whose borrowers were experiencing significant financial difficulties.

We provided a leadership service as opposed to the support service provided by the competition.

The partners of our firm actually worked the matters. Our entry-level staff people were partners and managers of Big 8 accounting firms. We worked in small teams of two or three professionals.

We built long-standing iron clad relationships with our clients through superior service and well-honed skills. That service was defined as solving the client's problem, both the bank's problem and the problem of the person who hired us.

We used an inductive methodology vs. a deductive methodology to perform our work. We used our experience and understanding of similar matters to decide what were the likely outcomes. We used this approach to decide what analyses were required and then what data was required.

Our reports were as short as possible by focusing on the important issues and information that impacted our client's decision-making process.

THE MARKET

At that time, the market was 10 years old and dominated by the Big 8 accounting firms. Each of the firms had a bankruptcy group that was a very small part of those firms. The Big 8 were actually focused on audit, tax and consulting services, not on bankruptcy services.

As a result, the firms were not set up to optimize the bankruptcy groups. The individuals who led these groups generally didn't start their careers with their current firms. In large accounting firms, this meant that the leader of these groups didn't have the same political support and power they would have had if they had started their careers at those firms.

THE BIG 8 MODEL

The bankruptcy groups followed the profit model of the audit practice. This model was based on the traditional pyramid structure that required and rewarded having the highest number of staff to each partner.

Partners were supposed to spend significant time marketing. Therefore they were expected to only have 1000–1200 chargeable hours each year.

Furthermore, the firms had the view that the optimum chargeability per staff person was around 85–90% of a standard 2000 hours. Beyond 90%, these firms believed that the staff wasn't taking care of other aspects of their professional career. But they spent 2500 hours in total anyway.

So, in the Big 8 model, large teams were assigned to matters and, more often than not, the largest amount of time and fees were attributable to the least experienced personnel. Therefore, the clients reviewed bills showing the majority of the fees for personnel that they usually didn't even know.

THE P&M MODEL

Our view was that the business required senior level advice that was primarily available from partner level personnel. Financially troubled businesses require experience and insight into every facet of business. In fact, we thought there was little value that inexperienced staff could efficiently provide to financially troubled situations.

Our firm originally had an upside down pyramid (this moved to a diamond shape and then a cylinder). Most of our personnel were very experienced. We sold a partner level service.

In fact, the profit model was driven by the partners being incredibly chargeable not by hoards of staff providing relatively little value.

We staffed our cases with small efficient teams vs. the large teams supplied by the Big 8. The clients knew everyone on the team so there was no surprise staff on the invoices.

Smaller more experienced teams were more efficient and provided more value in each matter. Generally, in each of our matters, our average rate per hour was higher than the Big 8 firms, but, our total fees were lower. This reinforced our vision to our clients.

CREDITOR VS. DEBTOR/OUT-OF-COURT VS. IN COURT

The Big 8 model was focused on getting the debtor/company side of each matter. Why? In any matter, the company advisors earn more fees than the creditor advisors. Further, additional services could be sold by the audit, tax and consulting practices. In addition, bankruptcy work vs. out-of-court restructurings would provide for longer engagements with larger fees per month.

However, this required a large marketing and selling effort to win new clients every matter. Partners were expected to spend significant hours marketing to prospective clients. This took time away from chargeable hours and from the quality of the service.

The Big 8 would usually go after the bank group and unsecured creditor work only after they didn't receive the company work.

We concluded to go after the secured creditor market for several reasons. The Big 8 firms preferred the company side and were organized to serve that market, not the bank market.

The banks knew that because the Big 8 would ask the banks to refer them to the company. Only after not receiving the company work, would the firms come back and see if they could work for the banks. What kind of message did that send?

Letting the banks know that we were 'bank guys' resonated with a group that was looking for a different service. Secured bank work had many benefits besides that the competition didn't focused on them as their primary client.

BANK WORK

Secured banks also paid fees on a timely basis. Unlike the companies, the banks did not have cash flow problems. They were good for the money. The banks also were generally the first group to recognize a potential problem.

As a result, being hired by the banks got us into situations very early. This meant that the majority of our work was out-of-court which was much better for cash flow and 100% collectable. Out-of-court matters have no judge, trustee or other parties who might unjustifiably object to our fees.

Over time, when the banks retained us, we would require that the borrowers give us a retainer that we would hold for the duration of the engagement. Then, the borrowers paid us monthly. As a result, our bank clients rarely came out of pocket to pay our fees. And, there was no record at the banks of how much our fees were in total.

CONVENTIONAL WISDOM

The typical professional services firm starts by renting an office, hiring people and signing up new work.

We, of course, went the opposite way. We went out and signed up the work first. Then we hired people and only then did we add space.

THE SERVICE

We also defined the service differently than the Big 8. It wasn't just the bank's problem that we had to address. We had to work to make sure that the specific person hiring us was properly supported in the situation.

This was definitely unique. Other firms could not do this because their senior people weren't working the case everyday.

Furthermore, we worked for agents of syndicated credits. The Big 8 defined their client as the agent. We defined our client as the entire bank group. This made a huge difference to our clients.

Participants are often skeptical of agents in distressed credits. We explained to agents that it was in their best interest that we keep all the participants informed on a timely basis. After all, in an out-of-court deal, 100% participation was required. It is much better and easier to sell a deal when everyone understands what is being done and why it is in their best interest.

We even helped the participants to sell the solutions to their own committees. This became especially critical as the secondary market heated up after time and the participants were constantly changing.

The Big 8 firms generally took a different approach. They narrowly defined the client as the agent and excluded the participants. This resulted in those firms alienating various participants, who were also potential clients, and didn't help to build a consensus.

Our approach also provided us an additional benefit. It became a great marketing tool. By treating the participants as clients, we spent quality time with each of them taking them through the issues of the day.

We were able to showcase our competence, build relationships and get paid to do it.

FIDUCIARY VS. ADVOCATE

A number of the ideas that were the foundation of the vision were based on the approach that Frank Zolfo had employed when he was at the top of the industry.

Fiduciary vs. advocate was one of those ideas. It was very consistent with my personality and critical to the vision.

Most firms and individual professionals viewed themselves as advocates for their client's position. They would fight for their client's position.

However, to me it seemed that getting a deal done, sooner than later, on acceptable terms, was usually the definition of success for our clients.

So, I believed that part of our role was to first get consensus in the bank group, then to get a deal with company and other parties-in-interest.

To build a consensus, we first had to make sure that each of the participants in the bank group had the same data. Too often members of the group would not have the same data and therefore came to different conclusions.

Further, even if institutions had the same data, they would often have different interpretations of the data. They would then also reach different conclusions.

We worked to get parties the same data and then the same interpretation of the data. This helped to isolate the true differences and allowed for better reconciliation of differences.

This fiduciary approach was unique in the marketplace and served us well to establish our position in the marketplace.

I believe this was the cornerstone of our service approach and it resulted in over 90% of our work being sole source for the first ten years.

HIRING

We hired experienced professionals who were adults. And, we expected adult behavior. I did not tolerate whining or politics. I insisted on grown-up behavior and teamwork. This no tolerance policy fostered a good working environment for the majority of our employees.

I also had concluded that I wasn't particularly good at hiring people that I didn't know. At our previous firm, the recruiting process would generally last for two or three months. It would include numerous firm people and several outside people. A person would be hired and a week after they started, everyone would know if it was a mistake or not.

I decided, therefore, to initially only hire people we had worked with before or that came very highly recommended by people we knew very well.

As a result, we usually didn't hire anyone who had ever done troubled-company work before. That actually was a benefit for us. We were able to teach people our way of performing the service without having to address the way they had previously performed the service.

COMPENSATION MODEL—ALIGNING INTERESTS

In 1988, I was working at Zolfo Cooper on Allegheny International the parent company of Sunbeam with Steve who was a subcontractor. One night Steve and I were working late. Around midnight Steve started whistling.

"Excuse me Steve. It is midnight. Why are you whistling?"

Steve replied, "I get paid by the hour since I am a subcontractor. So I am making money."

"Well, I don't get paid by the hour. In fact, my hourly rate is dropping every hour I work."

I filed that story away and brought it out when we started P& M.

I decided that a salary and bonus comp model was in conflict with a firm that billed by the hour. This comp model caused the staff to hide after busy periods until they became bored or found by "Staffing" personnel. Further, staff people get bitter when they are working hard on nights and weekends and the partners are home but making money off the staff's sacrifices.

And while the partners might say that such effort will be recognized in the year-end bonus, is it really? Is it readily identifiable?

I proposed paying the professional staff an hourly rate for chargeable hours and only chargeable hours. Then the staff's interests and the firm's interests were perfectly aligned. Now when the staff was working late or on weekend, at least they were being paid.

When I told my former partner that we should pay the staff by the hour, he looked at me like I was crazy. But after I explained the concept to him, he agreed and it was one of the keys to our success.

Sometimes comp is a motivator, but sometimes lack of comp is a bigger de-motivator. The method paid the staff currently for effort, not at the end of the year at bonus time. The staff, within certain parameters, could greatly determine how much they would make in a year.

There were requirements for this system to work properly that over time were not always apparent to the partners and staff. This required the firm to have a very high collection experience.

P&M in fact, collected over 99% of fees every year in existence. The partners needed to closely work every case so that the right work was performed efficiently. Also, the partners would then have a very good sense of the appropriateness of the hours charged.

This comp model also required sizing the firm so that level of work was at or above the level of hours available from the staff.

The hourly rate paid to each employee assumed some amount of non-chargeable admin and practice development time would be spent over the year. The compensation for which was imbedded in the hourly rate.

The staff was also responsible for their own professional development and keeping current on their Continuing Professional Education. Most firms monitored the licensing and CPE requirements for the staff.

My view was that they were adults and professionals and could do this themselves. We also did not hold ourselves out as an accounting firm so we had no legal requirements to do so.

This comp model actually made the staff owners of their own hours. Everyday they had to decide if they were going to be chargeable, do administrative work, be sick, take vacation or do practice development.

It was quite interesting to see how uncomfortable people were with this decision. Some looked at every hour as dollars and made very interesting choices.

Remarkably, although none of our recruits had ever been previously compensated in this manner, virtually every person we made an employment offer to accepted the offer.

THANKSGIVING

Dave came into my office the week before Thanksgiving the first year of the firm.

"Hey Mike, are we open the day after Thanksgiving?"

"Dave, as you know, everyday is a holiday at P&M. Yes, we are open."

"Should I work on the Friday after Thanksgiving?"

"Dave, you can do anything you want."

"OK, I will work then. Mike, are you working that day?"

"No."

"Why not?" Dave asked.

I replied, "I never work the day after Thanksgiving."

MANAGING CHARGEABLE HOURS

One of the great benefits of this compensation model was the management of chargeable hours. In the traditional consulting firm, the management has reports to use to track chargeability by person. There are numerous discussions with staff about chargeability.

In this model however, the management never has to chase the staff. In fact, we didn't have management reports to track chargeability. (We did have payroll reports that indicated the chargeable hours per person per pay period, but these weren't used to manage the business.)

You see, the staff doesn't get paid for showing up. They only get paid for chargeable hours. So, who would show up for work, not be chargeable and not get paid?

The staff figured out real quick that if they were not chargeable, they wouldn't get paid. Then they figure out that they should look ahead a couple of weeks and make sure there is work for them. So, instead of management chasing after the staff to be chargeable, the staff chased the management for work.

Consider the following dialog when FTI was doing due diligence.

Stu, the President of FTI, asked me for our chargeability reports.

"We don't have chargeability reports," I replied.

"What do you mean? How do you manage the hours?"

"We don't manage the hours. They manage themselves."

"What????"

"Stu, the people only make money if they have chargeable hours. Who is going to come to work, hang out, not work chargeable hours and not get paid? I don't have to see who is not working and go find them.

In fact, when they see that they aren't going to be busy, they are chasing me down."

"That can't work!"

"Sure it can. What is your average chargeable hours per person?"

Stu proudly replied, "1600 hours" (80% on a 2000 hr year).

"Well ours are 2500 hours over the past 10 years (125%)."

COMP AFTER ACQUISITION

When P&M was acquired by FTI, we expressed the plan to switch the FTI staff to the same hourly compensation model as P&M. Certain key FTI employees balked at this change. The key employee with the most strenuous objection was Cory.

Cory indicated that he was never going to switch to P&M hourly compensation model.

"So Cory, why won't you switch to the hourly comp model?"

"If I get paid hourly, I will feel like an auto mechanic."

"Is this a bad time to tell you that my father is an auto mechanic?" I replied.

"Is he really?"

"No, but what do you have against auto mechanics?"

"Hourly pay is not professional."

"That is not your problem Cory."

"Yes it is!"

"No, it isn't and I will prove it to you."

"How are you going to do that?"

"Just watch. If I pay you $1000 per hour ($2million for the year) would you switch to the hourly comp model?"

Cory immediately replied, "YES".

"See, I told that hourly pay wasn't the problem."

"The problem is that under the hourly comp model, you own your hours, therefore, you will be held responsible and accountable for all your hours. And, you don't like that because there is no way to hide. Go home and think about it."

Cory switched to the hourly comp model and saw his compensation soar for the same number of hours worked every year. Instead of wasting hours, he became very efficient.

The month the FTI employees switched to the hourly compensation model, chargeability increased 40% and quickly settled in at 50% higher than historical measures.

THE P&M PROFIT MODEL

Most accounting and consulting firms try to achieve the 1/3–1/3–1/3 profit model. That is one-third of revenues for compensation, one-third for overhead and one-third profit.

I didn't remember that being included in the 10 Commandments, so I assumed that we didn't have to follow it.

Our model was revenue as high as the market would bear, compensation at an appropriate level and overhead as close to zero as possible.

A majority of our potential employees came from Big 8 firms and they were advocates of the 'one-third' model. They insisted that their pay rate should be one-third of their billing rate.

My view was that the pay rate was not a function of the bill rate. Each rate was determined by a different supply and demand curve.

What we could bill the client for a professional was primarily a function of the supply and demand curve for P&M services. Our significant position in the market drove our ability to sustain high billing rates. What the individual professional brought to the matter was secondary.

What we had to pay each professional was primarily a function the supply and demand curve for that person's skills. What were that person's job options? What did that person make previously? That is a unique supply and demand curve that drives the compensation rate.

VARIABLE COSTS VS. FIXED COSTS

By compensating our people on an hourly basis, we turned our largest expense into a variable cost. As our business went, so did out payroll expense.

We initially also made as many other expenses as variable as possible. From rent to secretarial by entering into a flexible office suite rental.

Selling and Marketing will be addressed in the next book.

COMING ATTRACTIONS

1.   What does the Boss think?

2.   The Sleep at Night Factor

3.   Inductive vs. Deductive methodology

4.   A Sales Story

5.   What Didn't Work

6.   Al Mintz's Good Story

7.   Bud and Trucking

8.   Gitano—losing cash

9.   Gitano—BOD stories, two sets of books, corporate inventory, Q4 write-off, world's largest report

10. How to Evaluate Management

11. London's Management Questions

12. Wherehouse Entertainment returns

13. Briggs Toilets

14. Incrementalization

15. Kelly's and Economics

16. Andrew and Supply & Demand

17. Country, company, crisis

18. Voids

THE END

You can do anything you want to do. But first, you must decide what YOU want to do, not what your spouse wants you to do, not what your parents want you to do and not what your friends think you should do!

This is not as easy as you think. Most people don't ever stop to think what they want to do. It is really the vacation question again.

Look for something that you love to do, something you are passionate about; head in that direction. That is where the fun is and where success lives.

When you are passionate about what you do, there is an energy and level of enthusiasm that cannot be faked.

I wish you all the luck in the world as you pursue your dreams.

TESTIMONIALS

"A real page turner. I will finish it next week."
                              Former co-worker

"I really didn't want to read it."
                              Mike's buddy Gail

"I have had the book for two months; I can't wait to get to it."
                              Mike's long-time
                                    friend Joan

"I couldn't put it down!"
                              Mark Fogel, Mike's
                                    Editor

"I couldn't pick it up."
                              Mike's long-time
                                    friend Diane

"I am very surprised; I liked it."
                              Ann "Seve" Brienza,
                                    proofreader

"I didn't want to read it either."
                              Bob O'Shea,
                              Consigliere client

"Mike wrote a book?"
                              Mike's mother

"Sure, he plays a 100 rounds of golf, spends hours and hours on this book. But can he help around the house?"

Mary, Mike's wife

"I am really glad he isn't in London anymore. Now I don't have to listen to his stories over and over."

Finbarr O'Connor,
head of European
distribution of the
book

AUTHOR'S BIO

Mike Policano provided restructuring advisory services to the financial workout and bankruptcy community for 25 years. He started his career at Arthur Andersen where he spent 7 years. He then spent 6 years at Zolfo Cooper, a restructuring advisory boutique.

In 1990, Mike co-founded Policano & Manzo, LLC which specialized in providing financial restructuring advisory services on behalf of institutions such as JP Morgan Chase, Goldman Sachs, Citibank, Wachovia, Bank of America, Bankers Trust, BankBoston, Cigna and Met Life.

Mike worked on matters in the US and Europe from Arthur Andersen to Kmart to Xerox.

Mike retired in 2005 and currently speaks at MBA programs including Villanova, Harvard Business School, University of Wisconsin, Yale, London Business School and to professional firms.

48707420R00080

Made in the USA
Middletown, DE
25 September 2017